When I Was a Child

Andy Stanton & David Litchfield

Hodder
Children's
Books

For Nina Elliot – A. S.

For Katie, Ben and George – D. L.

HODDER CHILDREN'S BOOKS

First published in Great Britain in 2018 by Hodder and Stoughton
This edition published in 2019 by Hodder and Stoughton

Text copyright © Andy Stanton, 2018
Illustrations copyright © David Litchfield, 2018

The moral rights of the author and illustrator have been asserted.

A CIP catalogue record for this book is available from the British Library.

ISBN: 978 1 444 92886 0

Printed and bound in China

Hodder Children's Books, an imprint of Hachette Children's Group,
part of Hodder and Stoughton
Carmelite House, 50 Victoria Embankment,
London, EC4Y 0DZ

An Hachette UK Company
www.hachette.co.uk
www.hachettechildrens.co.uk

"Back in the days before you were born," said Grandma,
"when the world was a rose's dream..."

There was butterfly-and-daffodil ice cream.

There were people who knew how to fly.
There were elephants in the sky.

Back in the time before you came,
when the world was a grand parade,
there were colours that didn't fade.

There were kingdoms under the seas.

There were doors
that opened keys.

Back in the summers of long ago,
when the world married the sun,
there was music in everyone.

There were steps up to the stars.

There were dancing girls on Mars.

Oh, I wish you had known it as I did then,
when the world was a crystal jewel.
When the grass was ten feet tall.

Long ago, when I was a child,
when the rivers ran young and wild.

But the world grew up and the world grew grey,
and the world turned slow and cold,
and the rivers got tired and old.

And the magic shrank away.
And it's not around today.

"But it is," said Emily,
"the magic's still here.
I can show you how to see."

Take my hand and come with me...

...to the places I like to go,
to those places you used to know.

There are faces in the raindrops,
the world is a diamond string.

There is wonder in everything.

There are minutes that last for hours,

there are birthdays for the flowers.

...no matter how old you are.

There are answers to every wish,
there are horses who are fish.

There are heartbeats in the mountains,
the world is a blue guitar...

The world is
a spinning star...